THE PUPPY PLACE

LUCY

THE PUPPY PLACE

Don't miss any of these other stories by Ellen Miles!

THE PUPPY PLACE

LUCY

ELLEN MILES

SCHOLASTIC INC.

New York   Toronto   London   Auckland
Sydney   Mexico City   New Delhi   Hong Kong

No part of this publication may be reproduced, stored in a retrieval system, or transmitted in any form or by any means, electronic, mechanical, photocopying, recording, or otherwise, without written permission of the publisher. For information regarding permission, write to Scholastic Inc., Attention: Permissions Department, 557 Broadway, New York, NY 10012.

ISBN 978-0-545-34833-1

Copyright © 2012 by Ellen Miles. All rights reserved. Published by Scholastic Inc. SCHOLASTIC and associated logos are trademarks and/or registered trademarks of Scholastic Inc. Lexile is a registered trademark of MetaMetrics, Inc.

Cover art by Tim O'Brien
Original cover design by Steve Scott

12 11 10 9 8 7 6 5   12 13 14 15 16 17/0

Printed in the U.S.A.   40

First printing, April 2012

For Holly, finally!

CHAPTER ONE

Charles Peterson was having a bad day. A very bad day.

It had started first thing in the morning, when he couldn't find his math workbook. Why had he wasted all that time doing problems 17A through 22C for homework, if he wasn't going to be able to bring them in to show Mr. Mason? "Where is it? Where is that workbook?" he mumbled, as he threw things around his room. Two mismatched sneakers, a hockey jersey, his favorite pajama top, one of Buddy's chewed-up stuffed toys — he could find all *those* things. But not his workbook.

"C'mon, Buddy, help me find it," he said, ruffling the soft brown fur on top of his puppy's head. As always, just touching Buddy made Charles feel better. That was something he could count on, even on a bad day. He sat down and pulled the puppy into his lap to give him a real hug. "You're the best," he whispered into Buddy's ear, as he stroked the heart-shaped white patch on the puppy's chest. Charles couldn't believe how lucky he was to have his very own puppy. Of course, Buddy belonged to all the Petersons: to Charles's older sister, Lizzie, to his younger brother, the Bean, and to his mom and dad. But Charles was secretly pretty sure that Buddy loved him best of all.

Buddy usually slept in Charles's room. He sat under Charles's chair at dinner (well, maybe that was because Charles had a habit of accidentally-on-purpose dropping scraps of food for him). And when everyone was sitting in the living room Buddy would always bring his favorite toy, Mr. Duck, over to Charles first.

Charles had known a lot of great puppies in his life, because his family fostered puppies. (That meant they took care of them until they could find each one the perfect forever home.) But Buddy was the best puppy ever. Buddy had started out as a foster puppy, but when it came time to find him a home the Petersons had all agreed that he belonged with them.

Now, Mom appeared in Charles's doorway. "Hey kiddo, let's move it. You're going to be late for school."

"I'm looking for my math workbook," Charles told her. "I can't find it anywhere."

"Hmmm, is that what you're doing?" Mom asked. "To me it looks like you're cuddling with Buddy." But she smiled as she crouched down to sort through the mess on Charles's floor. "Isn't this it?" she asked, holding up a blue book.

Charles stared. How had he missed that? He nodded. "That's it."

Mom shook her head. "You'd lose your own head if it weren't attached," she said. "These days you can't seem to find anything." She handed him the book. "Breakfast is on the table. Hurry down."

The next bad thing that happened was at school. Every Friday afternoon, Mr. Mason put a list of words on the blackboard for everyone to copy down and study. Every Monday when they came in, the words would be erased, and Mr. Mason would give the class a quiz. That Monday was no different. Right after morning meeting, Mr. Mason said it was time for their weekly spelling test. "Did everyone learn last week's words?" he asked. "Take out a clean sheet of paper and number it from one to ten, then write down each word as I read it out loud."

Charles was a pretty good speller. While other kids were staring into space or tapping pencils on their teeth, he quickly wrote down all ten words. As usual, he was one of the first ones to finish — right after Amanda Bing, who was always first. He passed in his paper and got out the book he was reading. The class always had free-reading time while Mr. Mason sat at his desk and corrected the tests.

Charles had only been reading for a few minutes, but he was already lost in his book — it was about a boy who lived on his own in the wilderness and got to be friends with all the animals — when Mr. Mason tapped him on the shoulder.

"Charles," he said. "You're going to have to take this test over again." Mr. Mason held out the test, and Charles was shocked to see red marks all over it. "You missed seven words," said Mr. Mason. "Were you having trouble hearing me when I read them out loud today?"

Charles shook his head miserably.

Mr. Mason nodded. "Okay, don't worry about it. We'll test you again later this week. I know you're usually one of my best spellers." He left the test with Charles and went back to his desk.

Charles stared down at his paper. He still couldn't believe his eyes. How could he have made so many mistakes?

"Oooh, Cheese blew the test," Sammy whispered from the next desk over. Sammy was Charles's best friend and next-door neighbor. They liked to call each other Cheese and Salami.

"Shut up." Charles knew that was not a nice thing to say, but right then he did not feel like being teased.

Sammy leaned over to look at Charles's test. "Sneep?" he asked. "What kind of word is *that*? It sounds like a Martian word. Did you turn into an alien over the weekend?" He made antennas out of his fingers. "Murp-murp, take me to your leader," he said in a silly, high voice. "I come from the planet Veeba and we need sneep. Many sneep! Bring us sneep!"

Sammy giggled, but Charles didn't see what was so funny. He pulled the paper away from Sammy and stuck it into his desk so he wouldn't have to see those red marks staring back at him.

The third bad thing happened at recess. Charles was the pitcher in a kickball game against a bunch of third graders. His friend David was the catcher. That day, for the first time ever, their team was ahead — even though the third graders were all bigger and stronger.

Charles stood at the pitcher's mound, facing

Danny Stumpf, the tallest and fastest third grader of them all. Charles knew what was at stake. There were two outs and runners on second and third base. If his team could just keep the third graders from scoring for about five more minutes, the bell would ring, recess would be over, and the game would go down in history.

He squinted at David. Earlier in the spring, the two of them had worked out a system of signals. David was a great catcher because he knew every kicker's weakness. He knew which ones should get an outside pitch, or a slow roll, or a bouncer.

David flashed a sign.

Charles squinted again, nodded, and let loose with a bouncer to the outside. Danny Stumpf took three strides to the plate, walloped the ball with his foot, and kept on running for first base as the ball flew up, up, up in a long arc. It looked as if it might go all the way past the monkey bars, but finally it began to drop — about a mile from any of the second grade fielders.

Danny circled the bases, pumping his fists and yelling. He and the other two runners crossed the plate before Sammy, the left fielder, had even caught up with the ball.

The bell rang. The game was over. The third graders had won again.

Charles trudged toward the door, where his class was lining up. He felt terrible. Then David said something that made him feel even worse. "Didn't you understand my sign?" David asked. "Stumpf *loves* the bouncer. I was asking for a slow roller to the inside."

After that, Charles gave up hoping things would get better. It was a bad day, that was all there was to it. He just had to get through the next few hours of school, go home and eat dinner, and go to bed. Tomorrow just *had* to be better.

At the end of the day he dawdled at his cubby so he could walk home alone. He didn't want to hear what Sammy had to say about his spelling test, his failure as a pitcher, or anything else. When everybody had left, he slipped out the door and headed home slowly, kicking a small rock as he walked.

"Hey, Buckaroo, where have you been?" Dad asked, when Charles pushed the door open. "I've been waiting for you to get home."

Charles shrugged. He didn't even feel like explaining. But then his dad said something that instantly changed a very bad day into a very good one.

"We have a new puppy to foster, and I was just about to leave to go pick her up. Want to come?"

CHAPTER TWO

"We're stopping to pick up Aunt Amanda on our way," Dad told Charles as they backed out of the driveway in Dad's red pickup. "I heard about the puppy from her, and she insists on coming with us."

"What kind of puppy is it? Where did it come from? Is it a boy or a girl?" Charles bounced up and down on his seat. Already, he'd almost forgotten all about his bad day. How bad a day could it be if they were getting a new puppy to foster?

Dad smiled. "I really don't have many details," he said. "The only question I can answer is where the dog came from. Remember how we heard about all that flooding down south last week? Lots of pets were left homeless when people's houses washed away. The shelters down there have done everything they can to find each dog's family, but there are still some animals left needing homes."

"But how did the puppy get up here?" Charles asked.

"Aunt Amanda has an old friend named Bunny who runs an all-breed rescue," Dad said. "She takes in all kinds of dogs and tries to find them homes, just the way we take in puppies. Her place is sort of a cross between a foster home and a shelter. I guess Bunny has so many dogs right now that she just can't handle one more, especially a young one. When Aunt Amanda told her that we foster puppies, she couldn't wait to meet us."

Charles sat quietly for a moment, imagining what kind of puppy they would be meeting. Maybe it would be a fluffy Pomeranian. He'd always wanted to foster one of those. Or maybe it was a larger breed. Charles had loved Maggie, the huge Saint Bernard puppy his family had fostered.

"You okay, pal?" Dad broke the silence while they waited at a stoplight. "You looked pretty bummed out when you first came home. Want to talk about it?"

Charles shrugged. "I just had a bad day, that's all. I messed up in a kickball game, and Sammy teased me about something, and stuff like that." He played with the buckle on his seat belt.

Dad nodded. "Not every day can be a winner, I guess." He shook his head. "That Sammy sure does like to joke around. I bet he didn't mean to hurt your feelings."

Charles looked out the window. He didn't want to talk about it anymore. He just wanted to forget about his bad day.

Dad pulled up at Aunt Amanda's and she climbed into the truck. She was all excited. "I can't wait to see Bunny. I haven't even talked to her for months," she said. "It's terrible to lose touch with an old friend."

"You and Bunny go way back, that's for sure," said Dad. "I remember when the two of you used to chase me around the yard because you wanted to dress me up like a baby doll." He and Aunt Amanda chuckled.

Charles liked it when Dad and Aunt Amanda talked about old times. It was funny to think of his father as a little kid. The drive to Bunny's was over an hour, but the time went by quickly as he listened to them tell stories and joke around.

"This is it," said Aunt Amanda, as Dad turned the truck down a long dirt driveway. Charles saw a rambling old farmhouse with a big red barn. "The kennels are in the barn," said Aunt Amanda, hopping out of the truck as soon as Dad pulled to a stop. "I bet Bunny's in there." She headed for the barn just as a tall woman in jeans and a denim jacket appeared at the door.

"Panda!" yelled the woman.

"Bun-Bun!" screeched Aunt Amanda. They threw their arms around each other and laughed out loud as they hugged.

"Panda?" Charles asked Dad.

Dad shrugged and grinned as he stepped out of the truck to give Bunny a hug.

Charles wondered if he and Sammy would still be friends when they were grown up. He felt a twinge in his stomach when he remembered how he'd spent most of that day feeling mad at Sammy. Maybe Dad was right. Maybe Sammy really *hadn't* meant to be mean. He just liked to joke around, which was ordinarily something Charles really liked about his friend.

"So where's this puppy? Why was it so important for me to come see her?" Aunt Amanda asked, after she'd introduced Charles to her old friend.

"Ha! You'll see," said Bunny. "Come on in, everybody." She led them into the barn. "As you can see, I've got a full house these days." She waved a hand at the kennels that lined both sides of the barn. Charles saw dogs of every size and type — and heard them, too. The barn echoed with the noise they all made, barking their heads off as Bunny strolled down the aisle speaking soothingly to each dog as she passed.

They were all barking — except for the last dog on the row. She was not barking, but she wasn't quiet, either. She was howling. The little brown and black pup sat on her short legs, her long muzzle tilted to the sky so that her floppy ears draped over her back. "Awwwoooooo!" she howled, and the sound made the hair on the back of Charles's neck stand up. He had never heard anything so sad.

"This is Lucy," said Bunny. "This is the puppy I told you about."

"But," Aunt Amanda said, "that's amazing." She stared at the pup. "She could be Pepper's twin."

"I know!" Bunny crowed. "That's why you had to meet her."

"Wait, who's Pepper?" Charles asked.

"Pepper was my dog when we were growing up," Bunny told him. "He was part basset and part dachshund and part hound, just like this girl probably is."

"Oh, and he was such a character." Aunt Amanda laughed. "Remember how he would howl whenever you left for school?"

Bunny laughed, too. "Of course. And who could forget the cowboy-boot incident?"

"Ha!" Aunt Amanda said. "That's when we started calling him Captain Hook. Remember, Paul? Do you remember Hookie?"

By now, the puppy had stopped howling. She tilted her head this way and that, watching Aunt Amanda and Bunny, almost as if she were listening to their conversation.

Dad nodded and smiled, but Charles saw him glance at his watch.

"Oh, I'm sorry," said Bunny quickly. "We're taking up too much time with our old stories."

"It's just that I have to pick up the Bean from preschool," Dad said. "My younger son, that is. If we're going to take Lucy, maybe you'd better tell us a bit more about her."

Bunny nodded. "I wish I could," she said. "But she just arrived yesterday, and I really haven't had a chance to get to know her. All I can tell you is that so far she's been a total sweetheart, and I don't think she'll give you any trouble. Poor thing. I know they've done everything they could to find her family. I'm sure she misses her home, but I bet she'll cheer up a bit when she gets some love from your family." She opened the door to the kennel and stooped to click a leash onto the puppy's collar. Then she handed the leash to Charles. "Enjoy her," she said. "From what your aunt's told me, I trust you to find her the perfect forever home."

Charles knelt down to pet Lucy's soft, warm coat. She looked up at him with her huge brown eyes. Then she tilted her long nose up and howled.

I feel so alone. I lost my home and my family — I lost everything!

The mournful sound almost made Charles feel like howling himself. Poor Lucy. He stroked one of her long, silky ears, then lifted it to whisper inside. "I'll take care of you, I promise. You're safe with me."

Lucy snuggled against his knees and let out a long sigh. Charles hugged her close and felt her warm breath on his face. "I'll take care of you," he promised again.

CHAPTER THREE

"You did *what*?" Mom stood in the kitchen, her arms folded.

Charles and Dad looked at each other. "Um, we said we would foster this puppy?" Dad said, as if he weren't really sure.

"Her name's Lucy," Charles said. "She's really cute."

Mom raised an eyebrow as she looked down at Lucy. "Well," she said. "That happens to be true. She's adorable. Those ears! But we are supposed to have an agreement in this family —"

"Uppy!" The Bean raced into the kitchen and threw his arms around Lucy. He had fallen in love with the brown-eyed pup the minute he first saw her, when Dad and Charles stopped to pick him up at preschool. Lucy loved the Bean right back. Her tail thumped against the floor as she licked his fat cheeks.

You remind me of a boy in my old family, the one I lost when all the water came.

"She seems really sweet, too," said Lizzie. "Didn't Aunt Amanda's friend tell you that she'd be no trouble?" Lizzie had gotten home from her dog-walking job just before Mom came home, so she'd already heard the whole story.

Dad smiled gratefully at Lizzie and nodded. "I'm sorry, Betsy," he said, turning back to Mom. "I guess I just got carried away. Amanda was so excited about seeing her friend, and they were both so sure that this puppy was perfect for us to foster." He looked down at his shoes, then back up at Mom.

"Can we keep her?" Charles asked. "Please?" He sat down on the floor next to Lucy, pulled her into his lap, and began to stroke her ears. Lucy looked up at Mom with her huge, sad brown eyes. *Good girl!* Charles thought. Who could resist those eyes?

Mom sighed. "Where's Buddy? We'd better make sure the two of them get along."

"I put him in the den when Dad and Charles first got home with Lucy," Lizzie said. "I'll go let him out." She headed for the door, turning at the last minute to lock glances with Charles and give him a secret thumbs-up. Charles grinned back at her. They both knew it was a done deal — as long as Buddy was friendly. And Buddy was always friendly.

Lizzie was back in a moment, with Buddy scampering along behind her. "Buddy, look, a new puppy!" Lizzie said, as he bounded over to touch noses with Lucy.

Lucy struggled to get out of Charles's arms.

Cool! Another dog to play with.

A moment later, both puppies were chasing each other around the kitchen table.

"All right, all right!" Mom threw up her hands. "But get them out of here so I can get dinner started." Charles could tell she was trying to sound stern, even though she was smiling as she watched the puppies play.

"Let's take them out back," Lizzie said. "I wonder if Lucy likes to fetch." Charles and Lizzie always wished for a dog who would fetch, since Buddy sometimes wasn't that interested in bringing back balls they threw for him.

But Lucy wasn't interested in the ball at all.

What she wanted to do was sniff. She ran around the backyard, sniffing at every inch of it: the grass, the fence, the rosebushes, the trees.

"That's the hound in her," Lizzie told Charles as they watched. "Hounds love to follow their noses."

Buddy chased around after Lucy, trying to get her to play, but she ignored him until she had checked out the whole backyard. Then, finally, she whirled around and put her front paws down and her butt up in a "want-to-play?" pose. Her long ears flopped onto the ground.

Buddy put his own front paws down, tail wagging. And then they were off, tearing around the yard in a mad chase. Charles and Lizzie watched and laughed, and the Bean clapped his hands. "Go, uppies!" he yelled, jumping up and down.

When the puppies were tired out, Lizzie took Buddy inside while Charles helped Lucy calm down by walking her around the yard. He wanted to make sure she had not forgotten to pee while she was outside. You never knew with a new puppy. This would not be a good night for Lucy to make a mess in the house, not when Mom had just barely agreed to let her stay.

Back inside, Buddy still wanted to play. He pulled his stuffed toys out of the basket in the living room, shaking each one in his mouth as he showed it to Lucy.

The puppies were playing tug with Snake when Mom called Charles, Lizzie, and the Bean into the dining room for dinner. It was homemade pizza, one of Charles's favorites. He had three pieces, plus some salad that Dad said he had to eat. He was stuffed.

After dinner, Charles and Lizzie both helped clean up. Then they went back into the living room to see what the puppies were up to. Lucy lay on the rug, chin on her paws, all tuckered out from her big day. She glanced up when they came in, and the look in her soft brown eyes went straight to Charles's heart.

Buddy wandered around the room, sniffing here and there as if he'd lost something. "What are you looking for?" Charles asked him. "Where's Mr. Duck?"

Usually when Charles asked that question, Buddy would run straight to his favorite toy and bound back with it dangling from his mouth. But tonight, no matter how hard he — and then Charles, and Lizzie, and the Bean, and even Mom and Dad — looked, they couldn't find Mr. Duck anywhere. Mr. Duck had flown the coop.

CHAPTER FOUR

"... and we still haven't found him," Charles finished up, at morning meeting the next day at school.

"Poor Buddy." Mr. Mason smiled at Charles. "He must really miss Mr. Duck." Mr. Mason was such a good listener. No matter what you talked about at sharing time he always had a question or a comment.

"I think he does," said Charles. "He was kind of moping around this morning."

"Maybe you can get him a new duck toy," offered Hannah, who always tried to make everything better.

"Maybe," agreed Charles. But he knew that Buddy loved Mr. Duck just the way he was, even though the toy had no stuffing in his belly and his once-orange beak was sort of gray. Buddy didn't care, as long as Mr. Duck still had two flappy wings and a squeaker in his head.

"Well," said Mr. Mason. "Does anybody have anything else to share?"

Charles raised his hand again and started talking before Mr. Mason even called on him. "I wanted to tell a little more about Lucy," he said. "She's really sweet and her eyes are so pretty —"

Mr. Mason nodded. "Maybe tomorrow you can tell us more, Charles. But right now I think Ben had something he wanted to share." He pointed to the wipe-off board, where people signed up if they had news to share. Charles had not really noticed the other names listed there.

Charles knew that it was only fair to let Ben

share. But he knew that what he had to say about Lucy would have been much more interesting than Ben's story about visiting his aunt who was a dentist.

He slumped down, staring at the yellow stars on the blue rug where they all sat "crisscross applesauce" for sharing every morning. He tuned out Ben, and thought about Lucy. One funny thing they had learned about her last night was that she loved to sing. It had happened when Dad put on some music after dinner. When the woman on the CD started to sing, Lucy did, too! She sat back on her haunches, lifted her long nose to the ceiling, and let out a long, mournful howl that cracked everybody up.

"Well, I see someone has a future in show business," Dad had shouted over the racket.

"She's a natural," Mom shouted back.

Lucy howled even louder. She didn't stop until the song ended. Then, when a new song started, she began all over again. When the CD ended, everyone in the family took turns making Lucy howl by singing favorite songs to her. Her best duet was with the Bean, who sang "Old MacDonald." Lucy seemed to love the "E-I E-I O" part, only when she sang it, it came out more like "E-I E-I OoooooooOOOOOoooOOOOO!"

"How about you, Charles?"

Charles's head snapped up and he looked at Mr. Mason. He had been so lost in his thoughts about Lucy that he'd almost forgotten where he was. "Um, what?" he asked.

Mr. Mason smiled. "Did you hear the question?"

Charles shook his head.

"I was asking everyone how their writing is coming along — you know, for the contest?"

"Contest?" Charles had no idea what Mr. Mason was talking about.

"Remember, I announced it yesterday," said Mr. Mason, patiently. "There is a school-wide writing contest going on right now. You're supposed to write about a pet, or any animal really, that inspires you."

Charles did not remember hearing anything about a writing contest. He had probably been too busy thinking about his stupid bad day, and how Sammy had teased him, and all that stuff. "That sounds cool," he said. Charles liked to write, and he knew he was pretty good at it. He was a better speller than Lizzie, even though she was older. That was another reason it had bugged him so much to fail that spelling test.

"Well, there's still plenty of time," said Mr. Mason. "Entries are not due until the end of the week." He stood up and brushed off his pants. "That's it for morning meeting, kiddos. We'd better get a move on or we'll be late for Reading Buddies."

Charles jumped up, too. He liked Reading Buddies time, when his whole class trooped down the hall to Mrs. Schubert's kindergarten room. Each kid in Charles's class had a kindergartner for a reading buddy, and they would spend a quiet half hour looking at books together. Charles's reading buddy was Oliver, a serious little boy with big glasses. Oliver loved dogs as much as Charles did, but his family didn't have one because his mom said their lives were too busy for a dog. Oliver always picked out books about dogs for Charles to read to him.

"This one," he said that day, shoving a book into Charles's hands before he had even said hello. "Read this one."

Oliver could be a little bossy at times.

Charles sighed as he looked down at the book. It was Oliver's favorite, the one with "Ten Thousand Dog Facts!" He had read lots and lots of those facts to Oliver, week after week, and honestly he was just plain tired of the book. Plus, sometimes squinting at the tiny writing on each page ended up giving him a headache.

"Okay," said Charles. "But first, would you like to hear about the new puppy my family is fostering?"

CHAPTER FIVE

When Charles got home from school that day, he raced into the living room. "Did you find Mr. Duck yet?" he asked his mother. She was sitting on the couch, looking tired.

"No," she said. "In fact, I can't even search for him anymore."

"Why not?" Charles asked, plopping down on the floor to pet Lucy and Buddy. It looked as if Mom was having a bad day. Charles knew what that was like.

"Because now I can't find my glasses." Mom rubbed her eyes. "I am positive that I had them on earlier today. Then I must have taken them off and put them down somewhere and . . ." She shrugged. "They've disappeared."

"You'd lose your head if it wasn't attached," Charles said, hoping to get a smile out of Mom. He got one, but it was a very tiny one. He cleared his throat. "I think I'll take the dogs out in the yard," he said. He grabbed his backpack. "Come on, Buddy! Come on, Lucy! Who wants to go out?"

Charles played with the puppies for a while, throwing a ball for them. But Lucy seemed more interested in sniffing things, and Buddy seemed more interested in trying to get Lucy to wrestle, so Charles finally gave up. He sat on the back deck, watching the dogs play. He thought about the writing contest that Mr. Mason had talked about that morning. What was it that he loved so much about dogs? What was inspiring about Buddy and Lucy? He pulled a notebook out of his backpack and began to write.

Dogs
by Charles Peterson

Dogs are the best. They always make you smile. If you feel sad, a dog will always make you feel better. My dog, Buddy, is a perfect example. He always knows just how to cheer me up, with a wagging tail or a lick on the cheek. Another funny dog is Lucy, the puppy my family is fostering. She is a basset mix, like a big sausage dog with long, floppy ears. She likes to sing along when you sing to her. . . .

Charles wrote for three straight pages, but somehow he didn't feel as if he had come up with anything worth entering into a contest. He needed something special, something nobody else would have thought of writing. Maybe Mom could help.

. Charles got up. "Come on, you guys," he called. "We're going inside." Lucy and Buddy charged up the stairs and followed him into the house. Mom was in the kitchen, opening and shutting drawers and bending low to look under cabinets. "Didn't you find your glasses yet?" Charles asked.

Mom shook her head. "Not yet. Dad just got home, and he's helping me look, too. Where could they have gone?" She put her hands on her hips. "This is ridiculous."

"I guess that means you can't help me with my essay," Charles said.

"Not now," Mom said. "Maybe later."

Charles nodded. It would probably be better if he just stayed out of the way. "Buddy!" he called. "Lucy! Let's go back outside."

Both puppies followed him back out the door. Charles sat on the back deck again, working on his essay as he watched Lucy and Buddy race around.

Dogs
by Charles Peterson

What do dogs think about? Do they have emotions, like we do? I think so. I can always tell when my puppy, Buddy, is happy. He wags his tail and his ears stand up straight. It almost looks as if he's smiling sometimes. . . .

No, that was no good. How about:

Dogs
by Charles Peterson

Some dogs have lots of nicknames. I like to call my dog, Buddy, all sorts of things, like Bud-a-roo, Big Bad Bud, Mr. Bud, and the Budster. My friend Sammy sometimes calls his dog Rufus the Great Rufusini. My aunt's friend used to call her dog Captain Hook, but I don't know why. . . .

Charles looked up to see Lucy coming toward him, her nose all covered with dirt. "What have you been doing?" he asked. "Sniffing a little too hard?" He brushed the dirt off, and Lucy sneezed and wagged her tail.

Then her long ears perked up and she turned toward the back door. Charles could tell that Lucy heard something. Now Charles heard it, too. It was Dad's beeper going off. That meant there was a fire somewhere, and he would have to jump into his pickup and race to the fire station.

But Charles didn't hear the pickup start. Instead, he heard Dad's voice. "Where are they?" Dad was yelling. "Where are my car keys? I just put them down for one second, and now they're gone."

Charles sat up straight. First Mr. Duck. Then Mom's glasses. Now, the keys to Dad's truck. Why was everything disappearing lately? Charles stared at Lucy. He thought about the dirt on her nose. He thought about that nickname, Captain Hook.

Charles scrambled to his feet and raced inside, just in time to hear Mom tell Dad to take the van instead. Dad grabbed her keys and raced out the door.

Charles tugged on Mom's sleeve. "Mom," he said. "I think I know what happened to Dad's keys. And maybe your glasses, and Mr. Duck, too!"

CHAPTER SIX

"What do you mean?" Mom asked. "Did you find my glasses?"

Charles shook his head. "No, but I think I know where to look. I have a theory. I think Lucy's been taking things and burying them in the backyard."

Mom raised her eyebrows. "Really?"

"It just came to me," Charles said. "She had some dirt on her nose, and then I remembered about Captain Hook, and —"

"Captain Hook?" Mom asked. Now she looked totally confused. "What does Captain Hook have to do with anything?"

"Because he's a pirate!" Charles burst out. "You know, buried treasure?"

Mom sat down at the kitchen table and put her head in her hands. "I just want my glasses," she said.

Charles sat down next to her. "Okay, I can explain. See, Aunt Amanda's friend Bunny used to have a dog that looked a lot like Lucy. And when we went to pick Lucy up, they started talking about how they used to call her dog Captain Hook. But I didn't hear why. Then, I saw that dirt on Lucy's nose and I realized she must be digging holes and I thought, Aha. Buried treasure. Captain Hook. So Bunny's dog was probably a digger, too. Get it?"

Mom rubbed her eyes. "Sort of," she said. "I guess this means we probably don't have moles, either."

Now Charles gave her a quizzical look.

"Don't you remember at dinner last night, when I was telling Dad about all the holes in the backyard?" Mom said. "I thought it was moles and asked him to figure out what we were going to do about it."

"I didn't even think of that, but you're right," said Charles. He heard someone pull into the driveway. "Hey, speaking of Dad, I think he's home."

Sure enough, Dad had returned. "False alarm," he said. "No fire. Now, back to trying to find my keys."

Charles tugged on his father's sleeve. "Hey, Dad, do you remember why Bunny's dog was nicknamed Captain Hook?"

"Huh?" Dad thought for a second. "Well, I guess it was because he liked to steal things and bury them, just like a pirate. Good old Hookie."

"Ha!" Charles crowed. "I knew it." Quickly, he explained everything to Dad.

"What are we waiting for?" Dad asked when Charles was done. "Let's go searching for buried treasure."

"But first," Mom said, "I think we should put Lucy and Buddy inside. Who knows what that dog will steal next?"

Charles went to the back deck and called Buddy and Lucy to the door. "Don't worry," he said, giving Lucy a hug as he brought her inside. "Nobody's mad at you. You can't help it that you like to dig."

Lucy looked up at him with her soulful brown eyes. She tilted her nose up and let out a howl.

I didn't mean to do anything bad!

Charles laughed and gave her a kiss.

It didn't take long to find Dad's car keys. Charles headed straight for the spot where he'd last seen Lucy sniffing. He dug around in a loose pile of dirt under a rosebush. "Ta-daa!" he cried, holding up the keys a moment later.

"Well done, Charles," said Dad. "Looks like you were absolutely right about Lucy."

"Now for my glasses," said Mom.

They roamed all over the backyard, poking into every pile of dirt they could find. After a while, Mom threw up her hands. "I don't think they're out here," she said.

The back door slammed. "What are you guys doing?" Lizzie stared at them from the back deck. She laughed when Charles explained.

"I don't happen to think it's very funny." Mom wiped a smear of dirt from her nose. "In fact, I'm beginning to hope that we find a home for that thieving puppy very, very soon."

Lizzie joined in the hunt. "It's not Lucy's fault," she said, as she dug around near the old swing set. "Some dogs are diggers, just like Labs like to fetch and border collies like to herd. It's in her genes. Plus, she's probably insecure because of losing her home and family. Once she feels more settled in, she'll probably stop stealing things."

"Whether it's her fault or not," said Mom, "that dog is not allowed to be out in the backyard on her own anymore. When she needs to go out, one of you is going to have to take her on a leash."

"Fine," said Charles.

"Hey," said Lizzie. "Look what I found." She held up a pair of glasses, all covered with dirt.

Mom rushed over. "Oh, thank goodness," she said. She took the glasses and went inside to wash them off.

"Now, what about Mr. Duck?" Lizzie asked, hands on her hips.

It wasn't until after dinner that night that Buddy's toy turned up. It was the Bean who found it, hidden deep beneath one of the sofa cushions. "Duckie!" he yelled, pulling him out and waving him in the air. Buddy came bounding over for a happy reunion with his favorite toy.

Just before bedtime, Charles clipped a leash to Lucy's collar. "Come on," he said. "Let's go for a walk."

It wasn't completely dark yet, but the sun was down and the shadows were long. The evening air smelled sweet. Lights were on in people's houses, and Charles could hear the sound of a baseball game from someone's TV. Lucy waddled along happily, sniffing here and there. The retractable leash let her roam far away from Charles, but when he wanted her closer he could reel her back in like a big fish on a line.

Halfway around the block, Charles saw George, the Galluccis' black-and-white cat, sitting near their front gate. "Hmm, I wonder if you get along with cats," he said to Lucy. He let her sniff her way toward the kitty, ready to reel her in if she started to bark or chase. They got closer and closer, and George didn't run away. Lucy pulled a little harder on the leash as they approached, and stuck her long nose out for a sniff. Charles saw that her tail was wagging. Maybe Lucy and George would make friends.

Then Charles saw the cat turn around and lift up his tail.

It was not George.

It was a skunk.

CHAPTER SEVEN

"Lucy, no!" Charles tried to reel the puppy in, but it was too late. The skunk lifted its tail even higher, and then suddenly the air was full of the most horrible odor Charles had ever smelled.

"AwooOOOooo!" Lucy howled. She bucked and twirled at the end of the leash.

The skunk ran off, leaving its awful gift behind. Charles had smelled skunk before — but never like this. This was more than a smell. It was much, much worse than a smell. This was a terrible, choking cloud that made his eyes water and his throat close up.

Lucy's howls turned to whimpering cries. She pawed at her nose. She put her head down and rubbed it on the grass. She rolled over, jumped up, and started to howl again.

"Oh, Lucy," Charles said. "You poor girl." He felt so helpless. What could he do to help her? He sure didn't want to get any closer to her. He knew he was lucky not to have been sprayed himself.

"AwwoooOOOooo!" howled Lucy, over and over again. She flopped down into the grass once more, trying to rub off the horrible smell.

"Come on, girl," said Charles. "Let's go home and figure out what to do." He tugged on the leash.

Lucy seemed confused. She kept whining and pawing at her face. Charles wondered if the skunk's spray had gone right into her eyes. "Come on, girl," he said again.

It was a slow trip home. Charles had to tug Lucy along, and she kept stopping to rub her face in the grass, or to sit back on her haunches and howl. Finally, they arrived at the back steps. Mom flung the door open.

"What is going *on* — Oh!" Mom interrupted herself mid-question and took a step back. "Whoa, Charles. Don't you dare bring that puppy inside this house."

"I wasn't going to," Charles said. "I just wanted you to know —"

"What happened?" Dad popped his head out, then instantly made a face. "Oh, brother. Do we have any tomato juice in the house?"

"Tomato juice?" Charles tugged at Lucy, who was still howling as she tried to get up the steps. "No, girl," he said.

"To wash her with. It gets rid of the smell."

Now Lizzie poked her head out. "Oh, ew!" She held her nose. "Don't tell me." She turned to Dad. "Forget the tomato juice. Aunt Amanda told me about a mixture that works much better. It's, um . . . peroxide or something?"

"Call her!" Dad said. "Now." He turned back to Charles. "Did you get sprayed, too?"

Charles shook his head. He didn't think any of the spray had hit him directly, but he knew he probably smelled pretty bad anyway.

"Okay. Get her in the backyard. Just don't let her in the house, whatever you do." Dad put his hand over his nose. "Wow, that stinks."

"P.U.! P.U.!" yelled the Bean, jumping up and down next to Dad. Buddy stuck his nose out between Dad's legs, then hastily retreated.

Charles half led, half dragged Lucy into the backyard. "It's okay," he kept telling her. "It's okay, Lucy. We'll take care of you. Stupid old skunk. Mean old skunk. It's not your fault."

"It's not the skunk's fault, either, you know," called Lizzie from the back deck. "He was just protecting himself." She pulled on a pair of rubber gloves. "Aunt Amanda gave me the formula," she told Charles. "Mom is mixing it up right now." She held her nose. "P.U., does that smell."

Charles could barely even smell anything anymore. It was as if his nose was overloaded. But poor Lucy looked — and sounded — so miserable. "Turn on the hose," he told Lizzie. "I'll start washing her."

It took three baths with baby shampoo and three rinses with Aunt Amanda's special formula to get rid of the worst of the smell. Dad, Charles, and Lizzie were all pretty smelly themselves by the time they finished, and Lucy looked like a wet rat.

"Let's get all our clothes into the washer first thing," Dad said when they were done. "And I think we'll put up the baby gate and keep Lucy in the kitchen for tonight. If any of that skunk smell gets into the carpet or the furniture, we'll never stop smelling it."

It was late by the time Dad finally tucked Charles in. "Well," he said. "That was quite a day, wasn't it? From buried treasure to stink beyond measure."

Charles nodded sleepily.

"You know what I keep wondering? How did you get so close to that skunk without seeing it, anyway?" Dad asked, as he smoothed Charles's hair.

"Thought it was a cat," Charles replied drowsily. "Thought it was George."

Dad peered at Charles. "Did you?" he asked. "Hmmm . . . I think I'm going to call Dr. Shelton first thing tomorrow."

"Who's Dr. Shelton?" Charles asked.

"She's an optometrist," said Dad. "She specializes in eyes. I'm starting to think that you might need glasses."

CHAPTER EIGHT

Glasses? Charles wasn't sure how he felt about that. Mom wore glasses. So did Dad sometimes, just when he was trying to read something. And some kids had glasses, too. Charles looked around the room in school the next morning, noticing for the first time that three kids in his class had glasses on. Anna wore pink ones, Brianna had round ones made of silvery wire, and Taylor's were sort of brown. Come to think of it, Mr. Mason wore glasses, too. His hardly had any frames around them at all; they were mostly glass and very cool-looking.

"I think I may know what Charles has to

share today," said Mr. Mason, when they were all seated crisscross applesauce on the rug in the corner.

Charles stared at him. How did Mr. Mason already know that Charles might have to get glasses?

Mr. Mason touched his nose. "I can tell by a certain smell that you probably had a little adventure yesterday," he said, smiling. "With a black-and-white-striped animal?"

Charles felt himself blushing. "I smell?" he asked. He sniffed his shirt. Mom had washed everything he'd been wearing, and he'd taken a bath before bed last night. How could he still smell like skunk? How embarrassing. This was the kind of thing that you could get teased about for months.

Sammy elbowed Charles in the ribs. "I didn't want to say it," he said. "But Mr. Mason's right." He grinned. "It's not bad. Just a little whiff. I remember when I was little and Rufus got sprayed by a skunk. Our whole family smelled for months, especially when it rained — but we were so used to the smell that we couldn't tell anymore."

"My dog got sprayed once, too," said Merry. "He came inside and rolled around on the rug before we could stop him. P.U."

"I kind of like the smell," admitted Ben. He leaned toward Charles and took a deep sniff. "Aah," he said, smiling.

Everybody laughed, including Charles. Then Charles told the story of how Lucy had gotten sprayed, and about Aunt Amanda's special formula, and about Lucy's long bath in the backyard. "And it all happened because I thought the skunk was our neighbor's cat, George," he finished. "So now Dad thinks I need to get glasses."

Mr. Mason nodded. "Hmm," he said. "That would explain a lot. I have noticed you squinting at the blackboard. And that spelling test the other day —"

"Yeah!" said Charles. It had just dawned on him that maybe there was a reason he'd gotten all those words wrong. Suddenly, he felt a lot better. "Anyway, Dad's going to make an appointment with Dr. Shelton," he finished. "She'll check my eyes out and then we'll know for sure."

"Very good," said Mr. Mason. "Until then, let's move your desk a little closer to the blackboard so it's easier for you to see."

Charles was surprised how much it helped, being closer to the board. He still had to squint to see the words Mr. Mason wrote, but at least now he wouldn't make as many dumb mistakes.

After lunch, a fifth grader showed up in Charles's classroom carrying a note from the office. "Charles?" Mr. Mason beckoned Charles up to his desk. He handed Charles the note.

Dr. Shelton had a cancellation today. Picking you up in half an hour, it said. *Dad*.

So Charles was going to the eye doctor — a lot sooner than he'd thought. After that it was pretty hard to concentrate on his report about lemurs.

He met Dad out front. "What's Lucy doing in the truck?" Charles asked.

"Hello to you, too," Dad said with a smile. "I brought her along because nobody's home, and I didn't want to have to go looking for the TV remote or my checkbook or something later on. Plus, I figured I could take her for a walk while you have your appointment."

Lucy couldn't dig in the backyard anymore since she wasn't allowed out there alone, but she was still taking things and hiding them, mostly under the sofa cushions. Lizzie had found her math book tucked between two cushions that morning, and after breakfast Mom had seen an odd lump under the rug and found one of her sandals "buried" there.

"You smell, Lucy," said Charles, as he climbed into the truck. Lucy looked at him and shook her head, making her ears flap. Then she leaned over to lick him.

It's good to see you. Where are we going?

Charles gave the puppy a hug despite her skunky odor. Who could resist those eyes?

"I guess we all smell," said Dad. "I got some teasing down at the fire station." He made sure Charles was buckled in, then pulled out into traffic. "Now, you know there's nothing to worry about at the eye doctor, right?" he asked. "She won't do anything that hurts."

Charles nodded. "I kind of remember going once when I was little," he said. "They make you look at a chart with letters, right?"

"That and a whole bunch of other stuff, probably," Dad said. "She might even put some drops in your eyes. But the main thing is that we'll find out whether or not you need glasses."

By now, Charles was already pretty sure that he did. As soon as Dad had mentioned it, everything made sense: Why he couldn't find things. Why he couldn't see the blackboard right. Why he was always squinting and rubbing his eyes. And even why he'd missed David's signal during the kickball game. He still wasn't sure how he felt about wearing glasses all the time, but if it helped with all those things it would probably be worth it.

Charles liked Dr. Shelton's waiting room. There was a fish tank and lots of cool magazines about bicycling and rock climbing. Peter, the doctor's assistant, was friendly. But Charles didn't have to wait long before a short, round woman in a white coat came out to get him. "Hello, Charles," she said. She smiled at him and shook his hand. "I'm Dr. Shelton. I almost feel as if you and I have met already, since I've heard so much about you."

"You have?" Charles asked. "From who?"

"From Oliver, your reading buddy." She said as she led him down the hall. "He's my son."

CHAPTER NINE

"Oliver is your son?" Charles asked, as Dr. Shelton showed him into her exam room. "But I thought his last name was Yee."

"It is." Dr. Shelton pointed to a chair that looked like the one at the dentist's office, and Charles climbed into it. "That's my husband's last name. Anyway, Oliver may even be here by the time we finish. He usually takes the bus here after school." She sniffed. "Hmm," she said. "I have the feeling someone got a little too close to a skunk."

Charles ducked his head. "Sorry," he said. "I know I smell. It happened when I was walking Lucy, this puppy my family is fostering."

"Oh, I've heard all about Lucy." Dr. Shelton smiled. "Oliver loves your stories about her. He has been talking about her at dinnertime every night. He says she's quite a singer. I wish we could consider adopting her, but with my busy practice here and my husband's job that keeps him traveling, there's no way." She pulled her rolling stool up close to Charles. "Now, let's take a look at these eyes of yours. Your dad said you've been having trouble seeing things clearly?"

Charles nodded. "I thought the skunk was our neighbor's black-and-white cat," he admitted.

Dr. Shelton laughed. "I can see how that could happen. Well, let's get started, shall we?" She pointed to a chart on the far wall. "Can you read the top line on that chart?"

That was easy. The whole top line was just one giant *E*. But it got harder when Charles tried to read the lines underneath the *E*, as the letters got smaller and smaller. By the fourth line, he was pretty much guessing. "*G*?" he said. "And I think that's an *S*, and maybe an *F*. Or a *P*." He felt a little nervous, as if this was a test and he was not doing very well. But Dr. Shelton smiled encouragingly and didn't seem surprised when he said he couldn't read the fifth line at all.

Then Dr. Shelton had him read the chart again, holding a black plastic lollipop-shaped cover over first one eye and then the other. "We need to figure out if the problem is in both your eyes or just one," she explained.

Next Charles had to read some words on a card he held on his lap. Then he had to look at another card, with colored dots all over it. "Do you see any numbers in the dots?" Dr. Shelton asked, and when Charles told her he saw a big 6 she nodded. "Very good. That means you're not color-blind."

Whew. Charles was glad to know that at least he had passed *that* test. "What does color-blind mean, anyway?" he asked the doctor.

"Some people see color differently than others," said Dr. Shelton, as she wheeled a table toward Charles's seat. "They may see red and green more the way we see gray, for example. Dogs see color differently, too — did you know that?" She touched the machine on the table. "Now, if you can just set your chin right here, and look through these lenses, we can do some more tests."

The appointment went on for a long time. After Charles had looked through lots of lenses and told the doctor which ones made it easier to read the wall chart, Dr. Shelton put some drops in Charles's eyes. They stung a little, but he hardly noticed because she told him a funny joke while she did it: "What did zero say to eight? Nice belt!"

Then she shone a bright light into his eyes and looked into them with a special viewer. Afterward, Charles sat blinking while she told him that his eyes looked "perfectly healthy."

"The drops I gave you will make your eyes very sensitive to light," she said. "We'll give you some special sunglasses to wear when you leave. You won't be able to read or see very clearly for a few hours."

"Oh, well," said Charles. "I can play with Lucy and Buddy."

Dr. Shelton smiled. "I get the feeling that you love dogs as much as Oliver does," she said. She scribbled something on a piece of paper. "This," she said, handing it to Charles, "is a prescription for glasses. You are what we call nearsighted, which means you have trouble seeing things that are far away. Peter will help you find some glasses you like, and you should have them within a few days. I think you'll be very happy to be seeing more clearly."

Charles looked at the prescription. So that was it. He was going to be a glasses-wearer, like Mom and Oliver and Mr. Mason. He wriggled down from the chair. He had seen lots of glasses in the waiting room, and now he was eager to try some on and decide which kind he liked best.

Dr. Shelton walked him back down the hall.

"Mommy!" Oliver jumped up from the play space in the corner of the room and ran to his mother. "Hi, Charles," he added, as he grabbed his mother's hand. "Look, Mommy. Look who's here!"

Charles blinked and rubbed his eyes. Was he seeing right? There was Lucy, sitting in the corner. She thumped her tail when she saw Charles.

This is a nice place. Everybody's so friendly.

"Well, well, well," said Dr. Shelton, kneeling down to pet Lucy.

"I hope it's okay," Dad said. "Peter said I should bring her in because it was getting too warm outside to leave her in the car."

"Peter was absolutely right," said Dr. Shelton. She stroked Lucy's ears. "Hello, little smelly girl," she said. "Aren't you adorable?"

Yes, I am adorable. And I can't help it if I smell a little!

Oliver joined his mom on the floor with Lucy. "She's the best, Mommy. Did you feel how soft her ears are?"

Dad turned to Charles. "So?" he asked. "How did it go?"

Charles waved the prescription. "You were right. I need glasses. I get to pick some out now."

Picking out glasses was exciting, but Charles had something else on his mind. He looked at Dad, then down at Dr. Shelton, Lucy, and Oliver. He raised his eyebrows in an "are-you-thinking-what-I'm-thinking?" way. Dad grinned back at him and nodded.

But before either of them could say anything, the bell over the door jingled and a woman came in. Dr. Shelton stood up quickly. "Oops, that's my next appointment." She smiled at Charles. "Have fun picking out your glasses." She gave Oliver a hug. "We'll go home as soon as I'm done with Mrs. Mellersten," she promised him.

Oliver played with Lucy while Peter and Dad helped Charles find some glasses that he liked. They were round, with red wire rims. "We'll send these off to the lab with your prescription, and I'll call you as soon as they come in," Peter said.

Oliver was sad when it was time to say good-bye to Lucy. He hugged her over and over and whispered into her ear. Charles thought the two of them looked very happy together. All the way home, he and Dad talked about how perfect it would be if they could convince Oliver's family to adopt Lucy.

But when they arrived home, they found Aunt Amanda in the kitchen with Mom. "Guess what?" Mom said. "Amanda's friend Bunny wants to take Lucy back. She expects to adopt out a few dogs this week, so she'll have room soon. Isn't that great news?"

CHAPTER TEN

One week later, Charles sat on the stage in the school auditorium, looking out at the crowd. The Spring Concert was over. The band had played, the chorus had sung, the orchestra had screeched and sawed its way through three long pieces. Now it was time for the writing contest award ceremony — and Charles was up there with the winners.

He smiled and waved when he spotted his parents. Lizzie sat next to them with a squirmy Bean in her lap. Aunt Amanda and her friend Bunny were there, too. Charles pushed his new glasses up on his nose and waved again. He couldn't believe how clearly he could see them all, how easy it was to see the expressions on their faces and the details of what they were wearing. Mom had on her fancy pearl earrings, Lizzie wore a T-shirt that said "Life Is Good" with a picture of a dog on it, and Aunt Amanda was wearing red lipstick.

Even Lucy was there — not in the audience, of course, but out in the van in the parking lot (it was a cool evening, so it was safe to leave her in the car). After the ceremony, she would go home with Bunny. Charles would miss her, but he knew it was the right thing. After all, the whole point of fostering puppies was to find them good homes. And Bunny seemed like a really nice person — plus, she knew all about taking care of dogs. Charles just hoped she would love Lucy as much as Oliver would have.

Charles gave his family a tiny wave. Then he looked down the row at the other people sitting on the stage. Next to him was the first-prize winner, a third grader named Mandy who had written a story about a lion cub. Charles didn't know the second-prize winner, a fifth grader who had written about volunteering to help save sea turtles. The third-prize winner was Alexis, another third grader. She was biting her fingernails as she stared out at the crowd with big round eyes. Charles had not read what she had written.

Charles had not won first, second, or third prize. He had won a special prize, a prize made up just for him and Oliver. Best Team Writing, it was called.

It was funny how it had happened. Charles had tried and tried to write a good essay or story about dogs, but he had not come up with anything that he thought was special enough to hand in to Mr. Mason. Then, one day when he was reading with Oliver, they had started to talk about Lucy again. And somehow, they had ended up writing a poem together. Charles showed it to Mr. Mason, and — well, the rest was history.

Charles pushed his glasses up on his nose and turned to smile at Oliver, who had just scurried up onto the stage. "Perfect timing," whispered Charles. "They're about to start. How ya doing there, bud?" Oliver was probably pretty nervous about being up on stage. He was only in kindergarten, after all.

Oliver pushed up his own glasses and smiled back. "I'm doing great," he answered back. He didn't seem the least bit scared. He jumped up to wave at someone, and Charles spotted Dr. Shelton with a man who must be Oliver's dad, sitting right behind Bunny and Aunt Amanda. "Hi, Daddy!" called Oliver. A few people in the audience giggled, but Charles could tell they thought it was cute.

Oliver sat back down and grinned at Charles. "Guess what?" he whispered, bouncing a little in his seat. "In the car, on the way over, Mommy told me that we can get a dog. I've been begging and begging her all week and she finally said yes. We can adopt Lucy!"

Charles gulped.

"Isn't that great?" Oliver bounced some more. "She figured out that Lucy can stay with her at the office so we wouldn't have to leave her home alone all day. Plus, Peter can keep an eye on her so she won't steal anything and bury it."

Oliver looked so happy. Charles didn't know what to say. He had told Aunt Amanda that he thought Oliver's family would be perfect for Lucy, and his aunt had promised to talk to Bunny about it. But Charles had not heard anything yet. He had not told Oliver that Bunny had decided to take Lucy back.

Charles knew it was only fair that Bunny should have first dibs on Lucy. But Oliver had been wanting a dog for so long, and he would love Lucy so much, and his family would give her a perfect home. Charles felt a knot growing in his stomach. All he could do was nod at Oliver and try his best to smile. "It's great," he said. "But —"

Just then, Mr. Giffin stood up to welcome everyone and explain about the contest. Mr. Giffin was a fifth-grade teacher, maybe the coolest teacher in school. Every year his class got to do really neat writing projects, like spend a whole semester writing poems and stories about penguins, or mailboxes, or hubcaps. Nobody could make you as excited about writing as Mr. Giffin — at least that was what Charles had heard. He hoped he got Mr. Giffin when he was in fifth grade.

Mr. Giffin introduced the first reader, Mandy. Charles gripped his paper harder, knowing that his and Oliver's turn was coming soon. He barely heard Mandy read, or any of the other top winners. But after the last wave of applause, Mr. Giffin turned to him and called his name. "Charles Peterson and Oliver Yee are the winners of a special prize, created by the judges this year. They are Reading Buddies who wrote a poem together, and we hope they've started a new tradition and a new category for our annual writing contest."

"Come on," Oliver whispered, pulling Charles's hand. "We have to go read."

Charles got up and walked with Oliver to the podium. He cleared his throat and tried not to look out into the audience. "Um," he said. He looked down at the paper. He swallowed hard. Now he had a lump in his throat, to match the knot in his stomach. All he could think about was how disappointed Oliver would be when he found out that Lucy had already found a home with Bunny.

Oliver jumped in. "Our poem is about Lucy, a puppy that Charles and his family are taking care of," he said, in a loud, clear voice. "And guess what? My family is going to adopt her and give her a forever home. I can't wait." Then he read the first line. "Lucy is a fine young pup." He looked up at Charles.

Automatically, Charles read the second line, the way they had practiced. "She loves to howl and dig." He pictured Lucy, with her head tilted back, howling up at the sky.

He and Oliver read the rest of the poem, alternating lines until they reached the final two, which they read together. "Yes, Lucy is a fine young pup, as I'm sure you now can see." The audience laughed and clapped.

Charles heard Aunt Amanda whistle through

her teeth. He heard Dad yell, "Bravo!" Then he and Oliver headed off the stage, along with all the other contest winners.

Mom and Dad and the Bean were waiting outside near the back entrance, along with Aunt Amanda and Bunny. Lizzie had already gotten Lucy out of the van, and Oliver went right over to say hello. Mom gave Charles a big hug. "You were wonderful," she whispered into his ear. "I'm so proud of you."

Aunt Amanda ruffled his hair. "Great job," she said.

"But what about — you heard what Oliver said," Charles said to her, pulling her aside. "His family wants to adopt Lucy. And I think they'd be perfect for her. But Bunny —"

Before Aunt Amanda could say anything, Oliver's parents appeared. "That was a terrific poem," Dr. Shelton said to Charles. "And if I may say so, you look extremely handsome and intelligent in your new glasses." She smiled and winked at him.

Oliver's dad reached out to shake Charles's hand. "I'm Steve Yee," he said. "Nice poem."

Charles ducked his head. "Thanks."

"What did you think of Oliver's big news?" Dr. Shelton asked.

"I think it would be so great if you adopted Lucy," Charles said, feeling miserable, "but there's one problem —" He looked over at Bunny, and Dr. Shelton looked, too.

"Oh, you mean about Bunny taking her?" she asked. "We already talked about that, while we were waiting for the ceremony to start. Your dad introduced us to each other. Anyway, Bunny is absolutely thrilled that Lucy's found a forever home."

"But —"

Oliver's dad explained the rest. "Bunny wasn't going to be able to keep her. She just wanted to foster her for a little while longer."

Bunny came over to join the conversation. "But your aunt convinced me that it would be selfish of me, when these people want to give her a wonderful home. Anyway, I can't keep every foster dog I fall in love with. Then I wouldn't have any room for more foster dogs. You know how that is, right?" She smiled at Charles. Then she looked over at Oliver, who was petting Lucy. "Still, I was not completely happy about giving her up. But then I heard Oliver say that his family definitely wanted her, and when I heard that beautiful, funny poem . . ." Her eyes welled up and she brushed away a tear.

Dr. Shelton put an arm around Bunny's shoulders. "We told Bunny she can visit whenever she wants, and she said she'd be happy to take care of Lucy for us if we ever need a pet-sitter. It's all decided, isn't it?" She looked at her husband and took his hand in hers.

Steve Yee nodded. "It's all decided. Lucy is going to join our family."

"Really?" Charles asked.

"Really," said Dr. Shelton. They all turned to look at Oliver and Lucy. The boy sat on the curb with his arms around the long-eared pup. Lucy's tail thumped the sidewalk as she licked Oliver's cheek. Oliver's face glowed with happiness. Charles felt the knot in his stomach loosen and disappear. With or without glasses, anyone could see that Lucy had found the perfect forever home.

PUPPY TIPS

Dogs sure can get into some trouble when they get too close to a skunk. It's good to be prepared with a remedy like Aunt Amanda's. Your parents can help you research "how to get rid of skunk smell" online for the latest information. My dog Junior once got sprayed by a skunk when we were out walking in the evening. Oh, boy, did that smell. For months afterward, whenever it rained and Junior got wet, that smell was still there.

Another animal dogs sometimes cross paths with is a porcupine. It's not funny when a dog gets a face full of sharp quills! In that case, it's usually best to take your dog to a vet for help removing the quills.

Dear Reader,

I was in third grade, a little bit older than Charles, when I got my first pair of glasses. I remember one day I thought I saw a beautiful white goose lying on the ground at the end of the Dodsons' driveway, next door — but when I got closer, I realized it was just a big white rock. That was a pretty good hint that I needed glasses! I have been wearing glasses from then on, and I am very grateful for the way they help me see the beautiful world around me, the faces of people I love, and words on a page.

Yours from the Puppy Place,
Ellen Miles

P.S. To read about a puppy who disappears, check out ZIGGY.

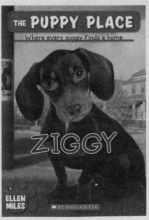

ABOUT THE AUTHOR

Ellen Miles loves dogs, which is why she has a great time writing the Puppy Place books. And guess what? She loves cats, too! (In fact, her very first pet was a beautiful tortoiseshell cat named Jenny.) That's why she came up with a brand-new series called Kitty Corner. Ellen lives in Vermont and loves to be outdoors every day, walking, biking, skiing, or swimming, depending on the season. She also loves to read, cook, explore her beautiful state, play with dogs, and hang out with friends and family.

Visit Ellen at www.ellenmiles.net.

KITTY CORNER

Where kitties get the love they need

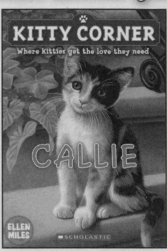

CALLIE

OTIS

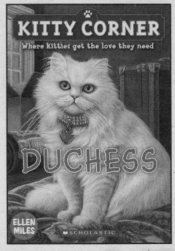

DUCHESS

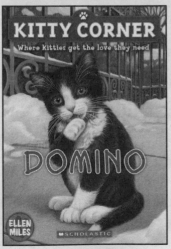

DOMINO

These purr-fect kittens need a home!